06-09-2012
Addison—
Your new baby
brother is so lucky
to have you as his
"big" sister!
Our love,
Nonna + Nonno

So you're going to be a ...

BiG
Sister

By Marianne Richmond

sourcebooks
jabberwocky

Mom and Dad told me I am going to be a big sister.

"No thanks," I said. **"We already have me."**

Mom laughed and told me a baby will bring
more love into our house.

"We have enough love," I said.

Then Dad told me a brother or sister is the best present
they can give me, because I will have a friend for life.

"I have enough friends," I said.

"We know this is big news," Mom said.
"We also know you'll be the
best big sister ever."

"What does a big sister do anyway?" I asked.

"Teaches what you know," said Mom, "and helps
take care of someone littler than you."

"I know **a lot**," I said.

"Oh?" said Mom. **"Like what?"**

"Chewed-up bubble gum is **great** for hanging artwork.

"Doll hair **doesn't** grow back.

"And," I said, "Mr. Tweeter next door does **not** like me to notice the spot on his head with no hair."

"That's plenty," Mom said and went to find Dad.

For a lot of days, my life was the same.
Mom's wasn't.
Her belly grew bigger. She started wearing stretchy pants like Grandma. She took naps and lost her car keys a lot.

She ate foods that **didn't** belong together like
potato chips in chocolate pudding and
peanut butter and egg sandwiches.

"What's with Mom?" I asked.

"It's part of having a baby," said Dad.

"I liked Mom the way
she was before,"
I said.

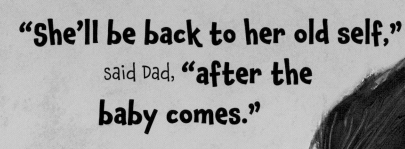

"She'll be back to her old self," said Dad, **"after the baby comes."**

"Where will the baby be?" I asked.

"With our family," said Dad.

"So things won't be the same," I said.

During TV time, Mom and Dad talked about baby names.

"How about Archie?" asked Dad. "After my favorite Uncle Archibald."

"Too stuffy," said Mom. "How about Daisy?"

"Sounds like a dog's name," said Dad.

The two of them got quiet.

"How about I-didn't-ask-for-you-and-now-you're-here?" I said.

Every time Mom did errands, she brought home diapers.

I counted 17 packs stacked in the corner of the baby's room.

"What's with all the diapers?" I asked.

"A newborn baby goes through 8 to 10 diapers a day," Mom said.

"That's a lot of *poop* for a little baby," I said.

"That's all babies do at first," said Mom. "Eat, sleep, and go potty."

"Borrrring," I said.

"You did the same things when you were little," laughed Mom.

"What does a big sister **do** when the baby's doing nothing?" I asked.

"**Lots,**" said Mom. "**You can hold him or her. Sing. Tell jokes.**"

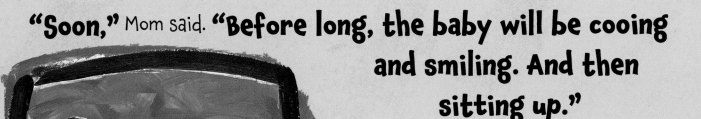

"**When does the baby get fun?**" I asked.

"**Soon,**" Mom said. "**Before long, the baby will be cooing and smiling. And then sitting up.**"

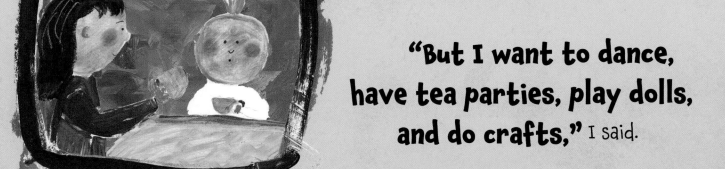

"**But I want to dance, have tea parties, play dolls, and do crafts,**" I said.

"You will," said Mom, smiling, **"just not right away."**

I found Bear and Blankie.

"Listen guys," I said to them.
"Mom said the baby can't drink tea for a while."

Bear looked disappointed.

We went to see Dr. Wald, the baby doctor. She rubbed a magic stick over Mom's belly, and "it" appeared on a TV screen!

"Strong heartbeat," said Dr. Wald.

"Hellloooo baby!" Mom and Dad said in excited, mouselike voices.

I tried to see a real baby in the kicking, moving blob.

"Hey..." I said quietly and half-waved.

Just then, the blobby bean's hand jutted out in a fist.

"**There's the pitching arm!**" laughed Dr. Wald.

"**He's waving at you!**" Dad said to me.

"**Or she,**" corrected Mom.

"**The baby sees his or her big sister!**"
said Dr. Wald.

I didn't know about that, but for the first
time since I found out about the baby, I felt
more happy than mad inside.

"Want to feel the baby move?" Mom asked me.

She pressed my hand to her belly. I felt a "thud, thud, thud" coming from inside.

I couldn't believe a real live baby lived in my mom's tummy.

"It's an alien trying to get out of a spaceship!" I said.
"Earth to baby, earth to baby. Show your face!"

"Couple more weeks," said Mom.

"How do you know when?" I asked.

"A mom just knows," she said. **"And you'll know when Grandma shows up."**

"Grandma smells like maple syrup," I said.

"You love maple syrup," said Mom.

Mom was cleaning everything in sight—curtains, cupboards, rugs, windows, and floors.

"It's called nesting," said Dad. **"Some moms do this to make sure everything is ready for the baby."**

"The baby won't notice," I said.

"Right," agreed Dad.

"And we're going to mess it up again."

"Yup," said Dad.

Just then, we heard her.

I woke up to the familiar syrup smell.

"Congratulations!" Grandma sang happily. **"You are officially a big sister!"**

"Really?" I asked. **"When?"**

"Middle of the night," said Grandma.

Suddenly, I couldn't wait to see **my** baby.
My important job had started while I was sleeping!
There was no time to waste.

**"After you eat, we'll go to
the hospital,"** said Grandma.
"Breakfast is pancakes with..."

"Maple syrup," I said.

I walked into Mom's room. She held a tiny bundle.

"Hey big sister," Mom said, smiling. **"I have someone who wants to meet you."**

I climbed atop the high bed.

Mom handed me a wrapped-up gift. **"From the baby,"** she said.

I opened a pink T-shirt with the words "Big sister" on the front.

Mom put the bundle in my arms.

The baby's eyes were closed. A tiny fist poked out of the blanket.

"Hey," I said. **"I recognize that fist."**

"What do you think?" asked Dad.

"I think he is...or she is..." I started to say.

Mom unwrapped the blanket to show me the color
of the baby's tiny T-shirt.

"**Lucky,**" I finished, "**to have me**
as a **big sister.**"

BIG Sister

is dedicated to
all the big sisters who
lead the way... —MR

Text and Illustrations © 2009 Marianne Richmond
www.mariannerichmond.com
Cover and internal design © 2011 Sourcebooks, Inc.

Sourcebooks and the colophon are registered
trademarks of Sourcebooks, Inc.

Published by Sourcebooks Jabberwocky,
an imprint of Sourcebooks, Inc.
P.O. Box 4410
Naperville, IL 60567-4410
www.jabberwockykids.com

Library of Congress Cataloging-in-Publication
data is on file with the publisher.

ages 4 and up

Source of Production: Leo Paper, Heshan City,
Guangdong Province, China
Date of Production: June 2011
Run Number: 15237
Printed and bound in China.
LEO 10 9 8 7 6 5 4 3 2 1

Also available from author & illustrator
Marianne Richmond:

The Gift of an Angel
The Gift of a Memory
Hooray for You!
The Gifts of Being Grand
I Love You So...
Dear Daughter
Dear Son
Dear Granddaughter
Dear Grandson
Dear Mom
My Shoes Take Me Where I Want to Go
Fish Kisses and Gorilla Hugs
Happy Birthday to You!
I Love You So Much...
You Are My Wish Come True
Big Sister
Big Brother
If I Could Keep You Little
The Night Night Book
Beautiful Brown Eyes
Beautiful Blue Eyes
I Wished for You, an adoption story
I Believe in You
Daddy Loves Me!
Mama Loves Me!
Grandpa Loves Me!
Grandma Loves me!
Pink Wiggly Pig

Find more heartfelt books and beautiful
gifts for all occasions at
www.mariannerichmond.com.